Running Back
Sporting Pride #1
Charity Parkerson

Punk & Sissy Publications

Copyright

—Warning: This book is intended for readers over the age of 18. Some of my books contain allusions to past abuse and trauma.

Contents

Introduction

*JAKK NEEDS SOMEONE TO **save him. Rocky needs someone to love him. Neither of them knows it.***

After getting publicly outed, Jakk finds his pro football career and the contracts he's secured in jeopardy. Thankfully, one of the biggest agents around has no problem doing what it takes to keep Jakk in business. Unfortunately, Rocky Zeal is every fantasy Jakk has ever had and a temptation he doesn't need. While there's no going back in the closet, he's equally not ready to be open about his private life. He's convinced that's the one move that will cost him everything. No one is more amazed than him by how quickly Rocky strips away the fear.

Rocky is more than familiar with Jakk's situation. He was in the same position once and lost his basketball career. Now he helps people like Jakk navigate the complexities of being openly gay in professional sports. It's something he feels passionate about. Of all the celebrities he's represented, Jakk is the only to get so far under his skin. There's nothing Rocky wants more than to believe Jakk won't destroy him. History has taught him that's the least likely outcome.

Running Back is the first book in Charity Parkerson's Sporting Pride series. These are sports-related romance, following men who find love while navigating high-profile careers. These are best enjoyed when read in order.

Chapter One

SWEAT POURED INTO JAKK'S eyes. Bodies slammed into him. The smell of the game permeated his nostrils. He was in the zone even though a fog dimmed his senses. Whistles were blown. Music blared. The crowd roared. Fireworks filled the sky. Jakk simply did his job on autopilot. Before long, water carried away the sweat. Eyes averted from him in the locker room. The second he could, Jakk headed out. Lights flashed in his eyes. People called his name. Jakk popped in his earbuds and kept moving. There was nothing to say. He had been outed right before the first game of the season. It was a nightmare.

Accusing looks and ugly words had been tossed his way. His agent's final words still rang in Jakk's ears. He couldn't sell a gay man in pro football. Not in these volatile times. It didn't matter Jakk could think of at least four out players off the top of his head. Brands didn't want his face. Maybe during pride month just for show. Otherwise, he was now a pariah. Jakk hadn't wanted this. He didn't ask for it. Living on the down low had worked for him. Unfortunately, it hadn't worked for his ex. Now that Eric had exposed him to the world, he supposed the guy got his wish. Everyone knew they had been a couple, but Jakk would be damned if he was manipulated like that. Eric had agreed to the secrecy thing. Jakk hadn't forced him. Then, the moment Eric decided he wanted the world to know and Jakk said no, Eric had decided he would simply make the decision for them. For whatever reason, he had been shocked when Jakk dumped him over it. The rage lived in his soul.

Jakk's feet slowed as his Mercedes came into view. A man beautiful enough to stop traffic leaned against his driver's side door. His khaki pants and tight polo shirt looked expensive. Jakk knew the guy's shoes cost at least a grand. His blond hair had the sheen of a man who spent big money on his style. He looked slightly familiar, but Jakk couldn't place him.

A million-dollar smile met his approach.

Jakk took out one earbud so he could find out who the guy was.

He beat Jakk to the punch. "Jakk Johnson."

"Yeah. Do we know each other?"

The guy straightened and held out his hand. He was tall. At least six-five. "Rocky Zeal."

The name tickled a slight memory. "Retired from basketball, correct? Sorry, I can't recall which team."

Rocky's smile grew. "Roadsters."

Jakk shook his hand. "Yeah. I remember now."

For a moment, they simply stared at each other. Jakk shook his head, shaking off the spell Rocky's looks wove. "Sorry. Were you waiting for me for a reason?"

"I hear you're down an agent."

The full memory of where he had heard Rocky's name overcame him. He was an agent who only represented the absolute best. His client list was the thing of legends. He never crossed Jakk's mind as even being a possibility for himself. Not that he'd had much time to think about what he would do.

Jakk winced. He likely looked like a true loser right now. "Yeah. It's been a day."

The sympathy that touched Rocky's features caught Jakk off guard. He couldn't stop staring at the guy's hazel eyes. Jakk had to tilt his chin up to hold his stare, and that was a rare thing for him. It was hot. "May I take you to dinner?"

Jakk blinked at the question. That was the last thing he expected. "Um." He rubbed the back of his neck. Jakk didn't know if the guy had just asked him on a date or what had happened. He had literally just left a long-term relationship like six hours ago.

"To discuss your future," Rocky clarified before Jakk had an existential crisis.

The pressure eased from Jakk's chest. He might have been outed, but he still wasn't ready to openly date anyone. "That sounds great." Once the relief passed, the truth sank in, and the excitement hit. Holy shit. Rocky Zeal wanted to discuss his future. That was an absolute dream. Jakk realized he had been standing there too long, internally freaking out. "If you'd like, I can drive. We're already at my car."

"That's probably for the best. I got here just in time to catch someone looking suspiciously like they intended to key it."

Jakk's eyebrows shot to his hairline. "You're joking."

Rocky didn't look like he joked. "No. He scurried away when he saw me headed his way."

Jakk swiped a hand over his eyes. "This is ridiculous." He dropped his hand and headed for the trunk. Jakk stashed his bag while trying to hide the rage. All night, he had been slightly numb. Now the shock of the day was starting to wear off, and the anger grew. His sexuality had nothing to do with anything. He was still the same athlete. This was exactly why he hadn't wanted anyone to know.

He slammed the trunk closed much harder than intended. Jakk bit back all the ugly words he wanted to scream at the top of his lungs.

"I know." The quietly spoken words pulled Jakk away from the edge and reminded him he wasn't alone.

His gaze moved to Rocky. There was real sympathy in his eyes. Jakk recalled something else about the man. He had retired at the height of his career after pictures were leaked of him with a man in a very compromising position. Tension drained from Jakk's shoulders. He hadn't even realized how rigidly he had held himself.

"Let's have dinner. I promise I can help."

Jakk nodded. For the first time in a long time, Jakk didn't feel alone. Rocky knew what it was like to be him. He needed that right now.

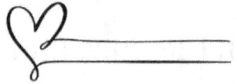

Fuck. The pain and rage written in Jakk's every line. Rocky felt it. The memory of suffering the same fate never faded. Rocky recalled every second of the turmoil, like it had happened to him yesterday. He would be damned if Jakk lost everything the way he had. Technically, Rocky made way more money now, but that didn't matter. The career he had loved and the talent he had spent his life perfecting had been stripped in one careless motion. Rocky wouldn't let Jakk suffer his fate.

When the news had quickly come down the pike, Rocky had jumped on the first flight to Minnesota. The adrenaline of the race had worn off and the exhaustion hit. Rocky did his best to power through. He was always tired. It was just another day. He had work to do.

"I've lived here for nearly six years now and I didn't know this restaurant existed."

Rocky glanced around at the observation. He spent a lot of time traveling all over America and Canada. Rocky was almost an expert at finding quiet places where stars wouldn't be bombarded. After all, that was who was always in his company, and his meals were always about business. "Yeah. I found this place a few years back when I signed Chipper Brown. It's a good spot for an uninterrupted meal."

Jakk leaned forward. His expression screamed excitement. "You're Chipper Brown's agent? I love that guy. He's the whole reason I watch MMA."

A smile tugged at Rocky's lips. He loved that stars still got star struck over other stars. "Yeah. I have an extensive client list."

"That must be exhausting."

Jakk's observation caught Rocky off guard. Most people never considered his comfort at all. He worked for them. They were the celebrities. It took a big ego to make it to the top. Rocky found himself smiling for real. "Yeah, a bit. It's worth it to me, though. I have a very particular talent. I know how to keep athletes exactly like you on top."

"Like me?"

Rocky nodded and tried to move on before Jakk could ask what he meant. He pulled out a folded piece of paper he'd kept in his pocket. Rocky unfolded it and read. "Since I'm not your agent." He paused for effect. "Yet. I don't have access to your contracts, so everything I know is what I gathered from research and public records. You've still got two years left on your contract with the team, so you're still good there. As long as you don't let this throw you off your game, they have no legitimate reason to release you. Unfortunately, your commercial deals and sponsorships aren't under any obligation to keep you." Rocky could tell by Jakk's expression, he hadn't considered any of this.

Rocky pressed on. It was best to rip the bandage off quick. "Like I said, I don't have access to your contracts, so I don't know if I have the full list. I also don't know the verbiage of what you signed. What I know from experience is, they almost always have the same legal language. You have to fall in line with their moral code. That becomes a gray area in this situation. My advice is to let it go if you get dropped. You don't want your name associated with a homophobic company anyway, so just don't sweat it." He glanced at his list and started with the worst. "With that said, Johnson Hardware will drop you. I've seen it. Each and every time, they will drop you. Greenway Cellular is a wildcard. They are known to change their logo to pride colors in June. Otherwise, they're pretty middling. They give donations to both sides of the aisle, so it's hard to judge. On the other side of things, Treadlong Tires will keep you. They love it. They're very well known for sponsoring Pride events all over the country. You're good there. Other things, such as uniform sponsors, won't get involved at all. They have too many athletes and are way too big to split hairs. It matters not at all to them."

"It shouldn't matter to anyone."

Jakk's quietly spoken words broke Rocky's heart. This part always devastated him. He set the paper aside. "Agreed, but until it doesn't, it does. It's not fair. None of this is right. You deserve to only be judged by your actions on the field, but that's not how it works. I can't promise any of this will be easy, but I can swear to you—if you sign with me—I will keep your career safe."

A sweet smile touched Jakk's lips. He was truly a gorgeous man. Rocky wasn't immune. It was no wonder some guy had tried to force him to go public with him. No doubt being kept a secret by this heart-stopping man was hell, but no one deserved what Jakk currently suffered. "I was ready to sign when we shook hands earlier. You didn't have to treat me to dinner."

A bark of laughter burst from Rocky. "Never be too eager to sign with anyone for anything. They'll fuck you every time."

Jakk's sexy, light brown gaze moved over Rocky's face. "Will you fuck me?"

Goddamn. Rocky knew what he meant, but still his mouth went dry. His nipples hardened as his stomach muscles clenched. Rocky never let athletes tempt him. Not anymore. He had never been more on board than he was then. Rocky hated to stay on topic. "You'll get a fair contract." There. He would be damned if said no to fucking him. That, Rocky very much wanted to do. He wouldn't, but the temptation was fully there.

Chapter Two

SHADOWS MOVED ACROSS THE ceiling. Jakk stared at each one. He assumed it was trees getting whipped by the high winds. His mind was a mess. He tried thinking about anything at all but his life. Unfortunately, his brain wouldn't stop and let him sleep. It was strange knowing he would never talk to Eric again. Truthfully, they had been over for a while. Jakk just hadn't wanted to accept it. They had been together for so long. He had honestly thought of Eric as his best friend. No one else knew him. Not really. That was why his betrayal cut so deep. He didn't hate him. Jakk understood Eric's actions were the last desperate attempt at saving them. Eric wanted what Jakk couldn't give him. He supposed Eric thought all that stood between them was Jakk's hiding. It wasn't.

For at least a year now, they had been limping along. Their fights had been epic for months, and then they had turned cold. The silence had set in and conversations stopped. Jakk had been holding his breath, waiting for the other shoe to drop. It finally had, and he felt oddly relieved. Obviously, he was enraged by Eric's actions, but he no longer walked on eggshells. Still, the room felt devoid of something that let him sleep at night. He supposed the feeling would pass.

A loud buzz brought his gaze toward the bedside table. His phone was lit. Jakk snagged it and checked the face. He smiled at the sight of Rocky's name.

Rocky: *You probably won't get this until morning, but I've put some feelers out for deals to replace the sponsors you lose. I've already gotten two bites. From my research, they look to be good choices.*

For a moment, Jakk simply stared at the message. He didn't answer right away. Jakk wanted to savor the feeling of not being alone. He also was a little stunned by his immediate reaction to hearing from Rocky. The guy was his agent, but that was not what he had felt like when Jakk saw his name. His first thought was *mine*. He had never been so instantly attracted to anyone. Obviously, he had been ready to fuck a lot of people in a heartbeat. This was different. He couldn't explain it. He liked Rocky. There had been a spark lit inside him at dinner. He felt seen.

Jakk: *Why are you still up working on my issues? I don't want you losing sleep over me.*

Rocky: *I went to bed and dozed for about ten minutes. Then the people in the hotel room next door obviously came back from partying. They have music blaring, and I'm pretty sure an orgy is happening over there.*

A smile exploded across Jakk's face.

Jakk: *That sucks. You could've stayed with me. I have plenty of room. It didn't occur to me to ask where you live. If I had realized you were stuck in a hotel, I would've offered earlier. There's a music festival in town. I'm surprised you even got a room, and you definitely won't be sleeping anytime in the next three days.*

A thought hit Jakk.

Jakk: *I mean, if you plan to stay that long.*

Rocky: *It had been my intention to hang around while we pan things out. I mean, I have something else I have to do for a few days, but I'll be back. I didn't know about the festival.*

For a moment, Jakk chewed his bottom lip. He didn't want to sound desperate. The house just felt so goddamn empty.

Jakk: *Come stay with me. Like I said, I have the room. It's quiet and no one will bother you here. Plus, we won't have to keep meeting up when you come to town, since you'll be right here.*

There. Hopefully, he sounded levelheaded rather than needy. As time ticked by without a response, Jakk second guessed himself. Maybe he had gone too far. He hadn't actually signed anything yet. Rocky could still withdraw his offer. It was possible he sounded like he wanted Rocky in his bed, which he did, but still. He hadn't meant his offer that way. Jakk wasn't that guy. His panic won.

Jakk: *It's okay to say no. I didn't mean to overstep or anything.*

Rocky: *Sorry. I was packing my things. Give me fifteen.*

Jakk's face hurt, making him realize how hard he smiled at his phone.

Jakk: *I'll be here. The code to the front gate is 5368. Come in through the side door. I'll leave it unlocked for you.*

Rocky: *Sounds good. I'll see you soon, and thanks.*

Jakk: *No problem. That's what friends do.*

The immediate cringe after hitting send was real. Maybe he shouldn't have added that last bit. He sounded like an idiot. His embarrassment lasted a half second before giddiness set in. Rocky was coming. Likely, he would go straight to bed, but he would be here. Under Jakk's roof. Down the hall.

Feet from Jakk's bed. Jakk could control himself. Possibly. Fuck. Maybe this had been a mistake after all. He smiled again. It was an error he would gladly make a thousand times. Rocky was hot as fuck. And a guy could dream.

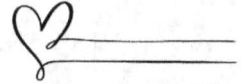

What in the hell was he doing? Rocky gripped the steering wheel with both hands, white knuckling it all the way to Jakk's place. What in the actual fuck was he thinking? This was insane. It was a terrible idea. He was such a fucking idiot. It was like he didn't know how to stop being weak. He couldn't get there fast enough. It was just a quiet place to stay. He was exhausted and had been for a while now. That was all. He needed rest. That didn't explain the way his heart rate kicked up as the gate swung wide in front of Jakk's house. He forced himself to focus on other things. It was a nice place. Not too big or ostentatious. Perfect for a single guy with money. Rocky parked, grabbed his bag, and headed for the side door. Jakk had said he would leave it unlocked, but it opened before Rocky reached for the handle. A shirtless Jakk stood in the doorway. Pajama pants hung low on his hips, showing off perfect abs and sexy obliques. Rocky needed to get his poor, neglected libido under control.

He pasted on a smile. "Hey. I didn't mean to wake you earlier with my text."

Jakk looked genuinely happy to see him. He stepped aside so Rocky could enter. "You didn't. I was staring at the ceiling."

Sympathy cut through him. "Yeah. I suppose it's been a hell of a day for you."

Jakk shrugged and closed the door behind him. "It is what it is, I guess. There's no reason you can't get some sleep, though. Come on." He motioned for Rocky to follow.

Rocky tried. Oh, God. He fought it. His gaze dropped to Jakk's ass. Fuck. It was perfect. This wasn't good. He shouldn't have come here. That was not what left his lips. "Thanks for letting me stay. Things were getting a bit uncomfortable back at the hotel."

Jakk glanced over his shoulder. His eyes swam with laughter. "I'll bet. I know my pitiful, newly single ass is in no shape to listen to anyone else having fun."

That wasn't pitiful at all. Rocky had to bite his bottom lip to keep from saying it.

Jakk turned left and clicked a light switch. "Here we go. There's a bathroom through there." He motioned toward a nearby door. "I'm pretty sure everything you need is in there. This is the room my mom stays in when she visits."

Rocky glanced around. It was nice. A simple guest bedroom with neutral colors. If Rocky had to guess, he would say Jakk likely hired a decorator to handle the place... or his ex. That was a depressing thought. He worked up a smile. "This is perfect. Thank you again." His phone chirped. "Excuse me." Rocky pulled out the device. A smile automatically pulled at his lips. "It's one of the brands I contacted on your behalf. I forgot time zones exist. It's likely morning there already." He opened the email and moved closer to Jakk so Jakk could read it as well. It was short, simply stating they were interested and would like to set up a meeting.

Jakk looked up, smiling. He was close. Too close. His eyes had specks of gold when the light hit them. Rocky was mesmerized. "That's awesome. You're obviously as amazing as I've always heard. Thank you for showing up for me."

Rocky forgot what they were talking about. He only knew Jakk thanked him. "It's nothing."

Jakk's expression shifted. He turned serious. "It's not. Today, I got betrayed and let down by people I had put all my faith in. People I had known for years. Who had been my friends and people I love. Yet you're the one who showed up for me, a complete stranger. You have no idea how grateful I am."

Yes, he did. No one had shown up for Rocky. He knew exactly how much he would have appreciated the support. Maybe that was exactly what Jakk needed to hear. "I do know because I was you." Rocky put some distance between them and set his bag near the bed. He didn't want to look directly at Jakk. "In an instant, everyone I had played with for years went silent and hid when we were in the locker room like I would molest them if I saw any part of their body unclothed. It was humiliating and heartbreaking. I felt betrayed and ashamed. Then, they cut me loose to save everyone from me—like being gay was contagious." Rocky sat on the edge of the bed and met Jakk's stare. Jakk watched him intently, as if hanging on every word, so Rocky didn't stop. "Everything was gone. No team would touch me. But an anger lit in me and kept going. It hasn't been that many years, but things are changing. Some people will accept you and I'll be damned if I let you end up like me."

Jakk crossed the room and sat next to him. Like Rocky had earlier, he stared straight ahead, as if he couldn't look at Rocky as he spoke. "I can't lose this career." He visibly swallowed. Then he turned his head, and their faces were inches apart. His eyes looked every bit as devastated as he sounded. "This is all I know. I didn't finish college so I could enter the draft early. That's why I've stayed on the down low. I made a choice for my future, betting everything on football. Yeah, I might have a few million to my name in various sources, but I can't live on that until I die. If I lose this, I'll end up on one of those where are they now shows, working at a fast-food joint."

A smile snapped to Rocky's lips. "You absolutely won't. If by chance you somehow end up jobless, which I won't let happen, I've been needing an assistant for years. I'd hire you in a heartbeat."

Jakk didn't smile as he hoped. His gaze moved over Rocky's face, studying him. "You really are amazing. Whoever you're dating is lucky as hell."

It was like getting punched in the chest. An uncomfortable-sounding chuckle escaped him with no permission from his brain. It was a nervous tic. "Yeah, no. I might be in Ontario tomorrow morning and then New Orleans by tomorrow night. Then California the next day. No one can handle that. At least, not anyone I've met. I probably haven't dated anyone seriously in like six years." His mind stuttered. Goddamn. Had it been six years? That was depressing. He swiped his sweating palms on his knees. "I suppose I should let you get some sleep."

Jakk stood. "Same. You came here exhausted and then I hijacked your time. Get some rest. You're welcome to stay as long as you need, and if you need anything, I'm right next door."

Rocky nodded. "Thanks again. Goodnight."

Jakk dipped his chin before leaving Rocky alone. He pulled the door closed behind him. For a moment, Rocky stared at nothing, losing himself in his thoughts. It really had been six years. He was the saddest of messes.

Chapter Three

FOR A WHILE, JAKK chilled in his room, trying his best to keep the house quiet. He wanted Rocky to have as much time to sleep in as he liked. When thirst won, he headed for the kitchen and spotted the door to the guest room standing open. In the kitchen, he found Rocky. Not only was he shirtless and in nothing but workout shorts, he was also completely covered in sweat. With his back to the hallway, he obviously didn't know Jakk was there. He chugged a glass of water at the sink while Jakk enjoyed the show. He was perfect. His entire tall body was all sinewy muscle. He was built for speed. Jakk had spent more time than he would admit reading about him online before finally falling asleep. Everything about him was impressive. The guy was in his forties and looked more like late twenties. Jakk's entire body responded to everything about him. Then Rocky turned and spotted him. A smile stretched his lips. Jakk's heart skipped a beat.

"Good morning. I hope I didn't bother you going out and coming back in. I had to get my run in before I lost my will." He chuckled. It was hot.

Jakk forced his tongue to work. "No. I didn't even hear you leave. In fact, I was just kind of chilling in my room, trying to let you sleep."

They shared a smile.

Rocky checked his watch.

Jakk had a minor panic attack at the thought of Rocky getting away. "What are your plans for the weekend? This is a bye week."

"I have a thing in Pickering. There's a weekend-long birthday celebration that happens every year for a very well-connected man in import-export. I've been invited and I can't say no. It's too good of an opportunity to network." He eyed Jakk for a moment. "I get a plus one. You should come." Rocky's smile returned. "In fact, it would be perfect for you. Considering who the man is, there's zero chance any press will get within miles of the place. No one there knows you. You'll be in a whole other country and free of all the drama. Plus, there'll also be tons of free food and alcohol. It might be fun."

Rocky had him at joining him for the weekend. But he was doubly in at the no press thing. Still, he didn't want to seem too desperate. "Who is this big wig?"

For a moment, Rocky looked slightly nervous. "Um. Well. It's Len Cattaneo's party. He's sort of the head of the Irish mafia. But," Rocky said, emphasizing the word. "That's exactly why you'll be safe from prying eyes, and he has several legitimate businesses that have been known to sponsor athletes in the past. Mainly his family, but I'm the agent of those family members. This could be good for your career."

Again, Rocky hadn't needed to convince him. The mafia thing was fucking wild, but he was still in. Jakk shrugged. "Sure. Sounds fun. Where is Pickering anyhow?"

The loud bark of laughter that burst from Rocky had Jakk's cheeks hurting from smiling. "Ontario." Rocky checked his watch again. "I'm supposed to catch a private flight in three hours. Can you pull that off?"

"Sure." Jakk was used to nonstop travel. "Just let me know how I should dress for this thing, and I'll grab my passport."

The smile Rocky wore matched the way Jakk felt. He knew Rocky was just his soon-to-be agent, but he was quickly beginning to feel like more. Jakk prayed it wasn't one-sided.

"If you want, I'll grab a quick shower and then help you pick out your clothes."

"That's perfect."

Rocky nodded and set his glass in the sink. "For the most part, it'll be casual, but there'll be a few things where you'll need to dress the way you would when you're getting filmed arriving at stadiums."

Jakk nodded. He had plenty of high-dollar outlandish suits. "I'm pretty comfortable in all situations."

"I can see that about you." The serious note to Rocky's voice warmed his chest. Jakk honestly didn't understand what it was about the guy. He got to Jakk. Maybe it was only because he had shown up when everyone else walked out. Possibly, his sexiness tempted Jakk. Likely, it was everything about him. All Jakk knew was he needed to check himself. Rocky was a professional. Jakk had been out of a long-term relationship for literally a day. They were not only a bad idea, but probably completely one-sided. Rocky saw him as a client. Nothing more. Jakk let the way Rocky had been vulnerable with him affect him too much. He needed to match Rocky's professionalism from here on out. Jakk was his client. That was all he would ever be.

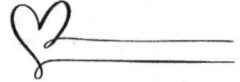

Rocky hated how much he liked Jakk. He recognized the thin ice he skated. Soon enough, Jakk would sign on the dotted line to be his client, and Rocky could not go where he wanted with Jakk. This was a professional relationship. Nothing more. But goddamn, he smelled good and looked even more delicious. He dressed the part of upper crust party guest to perfection. While Jakk shook hands at the door of where they would stay for three whole days, Rocky watched him with hunger. More than once, he forced himself to rearrange his features. There was no chance he didn't look as thirsty as he felt.

"I'll show you to your room so you can drop your bags."

Even as Rocky followed his longtime client and friend, Lennox Tremblay, it didn't occur to him Lennox had said "room." Singular. Then he stood in the middle of a bedroom, staring at one bed, and the reality of how this invitation must look to Jakk hit him. He knew what it felt like to be used. Rocky didn't want Jakk to feel like his contract hung on sex. He would never want anyone to feel that way. It sucked.

His gaze slid Jakk's way.

Jakk looked completely unbothered. He rolled his suitcase out of the way and hung his dress bags in the closet.

Rocky swallowed. "I swear I didn't know we'd be sharing a room."

Jakk glanced his way. His gaze slid toward the bed for a moment before returning to hold Rocky's stare. "It's no big deal. I can sleep on the floor or something if you're uncomfortable."

Rocky realized he was the only one making a big deal out of what was obviously nothing. He was stupid for not recognizing his attraction was one-sided and Jakk didn't even know his thoughts. This honestly wasn't a big deal when he looked at things from Jakk's perspective. Jakk wasn't attracted to him. They were adults and only guests in someone else's house. Likely, only one room was available and Rocky hadn't exactly RSVP'd his plus one. He couldn't expect more.

Rocky made a dismissive gesture. "That's not necessary. There's no reason we can't share." Except holy fuck. He would share a bed with Jakk tonight. That sounded like torture. It had been too long since anyone had touched him. Fuck his life. This had been a terrible idea.

"Lennox said something about dinner in ten. Are we dressed appropriately for that?"

Rocky shook himself from his inner panic. "Yeah. I guess we'd better head down." He could do this. Maybe. With copious amounts of alcohol.

Together, they headed back downstairs to a formal dining room. Several tables were also set up in an adjacent room, accommodating a ton of people. Rocky recognized several faces. He had a few clients there. They nodded as Rocky passed. Two chairs waited for them. Once seated, they were immediately greeted by their table mates. Rocky shook hands with the family solicitor. He was also Lennox's husband. They had worked together a few times on various contracts. Rocky liked him a great deal. He didn't hesitate to introduce Jakk.

Rocky motioned Jakk's way. "This is Jakk Johnson. He'll be signing with me soon. Jakk, this is Pierre Tremblay, Lennox's husband and the family solicitor."

Pierre shook his hand. "*Bonjour*. You've made a good choice in Rocky. What sport are you?"

Rocky couldn't help but smile at the question. He knew Pierre didn't follow any sport other than hockey, and only then because his husband played.

"Football. American," he clarified.

Pierre nodded. He chuckled. "Almost as violent as my husband's career."

Jakk's gaze slid Lennox's way. "I thought I recognized you earlier. It wasn't until we were headed back down that I remembered where I'd heard the name. Your team has done amazing these past few years."

Lennox nodded. They fell into a conversation about stats and whatnot.

Storm, the youngest of the Cattaneo's son's husband and another of Rocky's recently acquired clients, leaned his way. "Whoa. Good for you."

Rocky looked his way with raised eyebrows. "What?"

Storm's green eyes flashed with laughter. He exchanged a knowing glance with his husband, Barrett. When he looked Rocky's way again, his lip ring caught the light. He had always been a serious one. To see him enjoying a laugh at Rocky's expense actually warmed his heart. "Don't tell me. Just friends." He used air quotes and Rocky unexpectedly fought a blush.

Barrett and Storm burst into laughter.

Heads turned their way.

Thankfully, Storm was immediately distracted by the oldest Cattaneo son's wife dumping a baby in his lap.

"Here. We have plenty."

Storm beamed. He loved kids.

Rocky went back to focusing on Jakk.

Jakk stared at him.

For a moment, Rocky wondered if he had heard the exchange.

Jakk's gorgeous gaze moved over his face, as if searching for something. "Are you okay?"

At that moment, Rocky realized something truly unfortunate. For whatever reason, Jakk truly cared, and Rocky was so incredibly screwed.

Chapter Four

JAKK WAS HAVING A much better time than
expected. He hadn't expected to have a
bad time. Jakk had simply thought he
would be uncomfortable while staying with
someone he didn't know and surrounded
by strangers. Instead, he was made to feel
like part of the family. Plus, there were
a few hockey players present, giving him
someone to chat with about sports. Even
without all that, the alcohol flowed freely
and Rocky had been right. He didn't have to
guard himself here. Except he had to check

his longing. Goddamn. He couldn't stop watching Rocky. The guy was just gorgeous.

After dinner, they had changed into more comfortable clothes for music and dancing in the garden. Rocky cut loose, so he followed suit. He had laughed so much, his throat hurt, and smiled so much, his cheeks ached. His head swam with liquor, diluting his blood. When the music slowed, his inhibitions were already gone.

"Dance with me."

Rocky looked surprised by the demand, but he immediately set his cup aside.

Jakk led him to the wooden platform in the center of the garden that was made for dancing. The moment he towed Rocky into his arms, he knew he had made a mistake. He didn't stop.

"You surprise me."

The remark stumped Jakk. "How so?"

He felt more than saw Rocky shrug. "It's been less than seventy-two hours since you were outed against your will, and still, you didn't hesitate to ask me to dance. A man. In front of all these people."

"It's probably the alcohol."

Rocky chuckled. The sound caressed his ear and made goosebumps rise on his skin.

"Thank you for coming with me this weekend. If you weren't here, I'd be headed upstairs right now to avoid standing on the sidelines while everyone else got cozy. Not really sure why I just admitted that."

"It's probably the alcohol," Jakk repeated, making Rocky laugh.

"Maybe. I think it's just you, though." Rocky hesitated.

Jakk held his breath. He wanted to hear Rocky's thoughts more than he wanted his next heartbeat.

Rocky blew out a shaky-sounding breath. "I think you just have something special about you that makes people confess all their thoughts. That shit I told you about losing my career. I don't think I've said any of that to anyone other than my therapist."

"It was pity." Jakk didn't want Rocky to feel like he had dumped on him. He had needed to hear everything Rocky confessed about his career. Jakk took a breath. He could be vulnerable too. "I needed to hear everything you said right when you said it. No one else could understand how alone I felt yesterday." Something about slow dancing made Jakk feel like they were alone. Intimate. They could talk about anything. "I hope this isn't just a job for you. It sounds a little stupid, but I feel like I've known you forever. I feel like you're a friend." A friend Jakk wanted so much more with.

Rocky leaned away and met his stare. He looked like he took their conversation seriously. "I asked you to join me for the weekend after just meeting you. How crazy is that? Like I said, there's something about you."

Jakk nodded, and they went back to focusing on their dance. Somehow, they ended up closer. The music stayed slow and turned sultry. He didn't know what anyone else did around them. All Jakk could focus on was Rocky's body beneath his hands. His every breath turned shallower by the second. The air thickened. He had already gone out on a limb. Jakk didn't think he could be the one to take things any further, but he wanted to go deeper. He wanted everything.

Rocky's hand swept down his torso before slipping beneath his shirt. Jakk didn't even know what his feet did. His entire being was focused on that hand and the ragged way Rocky breathed against his ear. Jakk's dick was so hard, he couldn't think.

"I'm sorry." Rocky's hand fell away. "I shouldn't have—"

Jakk turned his head and touched his lips to the corner of Rocky's mouth, cutting off his apology. It was like the universe held its breath. Then their tongues were dancing and Jakk's knees weakened. One second, he explored Rocky's mouth. The next, Rocky held his hand, leading him through the house. He didn't see a single face as they passed. All Jakk knew was he couldn't get back to their room fast enough. He needed Rocky to touch him. Jakk might die if he didn't.

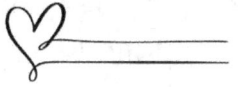

A haze coated Rocky's vision. He knew he was too drunk to make this decision. If he didn't take this chance, he would never forgive himself. At the moment, the consequences mattered not at all. He felt too much. Rocky couldn't stop. Tomorrow, he would feel all the regret. Tonight, he couldn't stop.

As his feet crossed the threshold of their assigned bedroom, he almost backtracked. Then Jakk's mouth covered his and his hands were everywhere. Rocky had worried he wouldn't survive the temptation of sharing a bed. He hadn't even made it that long. Rocky wanted this.

He tore at Jakk's clothes. He wanted to touch the body he had lusted over last night. His fingers itched to touch that bare stomach again. Fuck, he was so goddamn turned on by the thickness of Jakk's stomach that still managed to have defined abs. He knew Jakk hit hard when he took people down on the field. Rocky wanted to control that strength. The need to hear how Jakk sounded when he came was nearly crippling.

They landed on the bed. Rocky didn't care how they got there. He was too focused on tasting Jakk's tongue and exploring his body. Rocky knew he should slow down. Think. He couldn't. His soul ached for more—like it recognized its other half. Everything about the situation was insane. He had no idea why he felt so close to Jakk. Jakk was right, though. It was like they had known each other forever. He felt like way more than a talent Rocky wanted signed. This was way more.

Oddly, once they were nude, they didn't rush. Their hands explored while they learned each other's kiss. Jakk liked to use his tongue. That was more than evident by the way he toyed with Rocky's tongue.

"I hate that I'm saying this, but I don't have anything with me. Obviously, I didn't see this coming, and I was always faithful to Eric."

Rocky fought a wince at Jakk saying another man's name. Unfortunately, his words made Rocky realize this wasn't going farther. "I don't have anything either. My life is way too busy for any sort of relationship. I don't try."

Jakk nodded, brushing noses with Rocky with the motion. "Don't worry. You still won't be disappointed."

Goddamn. Rocky didn't doubt that for a second. Still, he wasn't the type to relax and enjoy. He was a doer. Rocky rolled. His mouth found Jakk's neck. He sucked. The sound Jakk made told him everything he needed to know. Jakk was definitely a neck guy. Rocky used that knowledge to his advantage. He licked and bit, sucking and teasing as he stroked Jakk's cock. Jakk writhed beneath him. His every breath shook as if he could blow any second. It was the hottest experience of Rocky's life. Jakk acted like no one had ever pleasured him—like this was his first orgasm and he didn't know how to handle it. His ragged breathing combined with moans. Rocky gave him the handjob of a lifetime, watching the sweat bead on Jakk's skin. He wasn't even sure if he cared if he got off any longer. Jakk was a whole-ass show—like watching porn. He openly struggled, fucking Rocky's fist. The way his tremors shook his torso as he took what he needed had Rocky ready to blow just from watching. Goddamn. No one else would ever top this and Rocky hadn't even gotten inside him.

Rocky barely had time to savor the satisfaction when Jakk's cock finally spit all over him. The world flipped. His back hit the mattress with a thump. Rocky's dick hit the back of Jakk's throat. A loud noise burst from him. It was out of his control. He didn't even know if it was a cry, moan, or if he begged. Maybe all three at once. It had been so long. So goddamn long since he let go of his ironclad control and stopped running long enough to let anyone touch him. Maybe he had simply forgotten how fucking amazing it felt to get blown. Rocky didn't think that was it. It was Jakk. He truly did love using his tongue. Holy shit. Rocky might not survive.

He scratched at the covers. Rocky strained with everything he had. He wondered if his heart would give out. An orgasm was right there, threatening to take his sanity. Then Jakk stroked his stomach lovingly at the same time his throat squeezed his dick. The world slipped away and there was nothing but ecstasy. He had no clue what he did or said. Jakk completely owned Rocky in that moment.

Jakk's mouth covered his again. Their tongues played lazily. Something cracked inside Rocky as their fingers linked and breath mixed. He very much feared it was the walls he had built around his heart years ago to survive. This man would be his undoing. Rocky already saw how it would end. With Rocky clutching the remnants of his tattered heart, while Jakk never looked back. Rocky had played this game before. He always lost.

Chapter Five

TRUTH BE TOLD, JAKK had expected the rest of the weekend to be awkward after an unexpected drunken encounter. It wasn't. Just as he had confessed—much to his horror—Rocky felt like he had been his friend forever. While they didn't feel uncomfortable to him, they also didn't talk about what was obviously happening between them. They also fully enjoyed sharing a bed for the entire weekend. Still, they hadn't had access to condoms. He was dying to ride Rocky's dick. Jakk wasn't sure it would happen. Soon enough, they would head their separate ways.

"Where are you headed next?"

Rocky glanced his way at the question. They were only thirty minutes out from landing in Minneapolis. Soon Jakk would be home, and he would only see Rocky when he signed his contract. He would be Rocky's client and Rocky wouldn't likely touch him again.

"Back home to New York. I have to meet with my attorney to get your contract sorted and I have a meeting scheduled with Oakley Wilkes to go over his convention deals."

"Oakley Wilkes? The retired baseball player?"

Rocky nodded. "He was the first player to take a chance on me. So now I do everything possible to keep the money flowing his way, even with his retirement."

"That's nice of you."

Rocky's gaze moved over Jakk's face. He looked serious. Jakk had a bad feeling he was about to get the talk. In a way, he was right. "You know I travel nonstop."

Jakk nodded. Things weren't exactly cut and dry with him either. "You know, I just left a long-term relationship."

Rocky nodded. "I don't have to leave for New York until tomorrow."

Jakk bit the inside of his cheek to keep from smiling like an idiot. "You should stay at my place."

A bright smile lit Rocky's face. "I'd like that."

"Me too." It was wrong how happy he felt. Jakk had been with Eric for six years. They had met on the first day of college and had been together through everything. Then the resentment had set in on both sides and the love died on Jakk's end. He had been going through the motions for a long time, trying hard to hang on to what he thought they would be. Plus, Eric had uprooted his life and gave up college to come with Jakk. Eric had risked everything on him. Jakk hated himself every time he thought about it. He didn't deserve to be happy with someone else. But then there was the rage. Throughout everything, Jakk hadn't once strayed or betrayed him. Eric couldn't say the same. Goddamn it. Jakk wouldn't let the past ruin the future. Plus, what the fuck? It wasn't like he had a future with Rocky. This was just a mutual attraction. Nothing more.

"If you've changed your mind, I'll understand."

Rocky's quietly spoken words dragged Jakk from the edge. He focused on Rocky. His intensity didn't let up, no matter how hard he fought it. "No. That thought never crossed my mind." He hated to lie, but he couldn't let Rocky think the sudden dip in mood was his fault in any way. "I guess it just hit me. I'll be back to the stress of it all soon. It was nice to pretend all this bullshit didn't wait for me."

"I might not be present, but I'll always be around. Just pick up the phone. Don't let this beat you, and—for fuck's sake—remember what I said. Don't let this interfere with your game. If you do, they win."

Jakk smiled. "Don't worry. I'm a different person on the field."

Rocky leaned his way and held his stare. "Don't be so sure. I've seen that intensity and passion off the field."

Goddamn. Rocky made Jakk hot in every way. He couldn't wait to show him exactly how passionate he could be.

By the time the plane landed, and they were loaded in Jakk's car, Jakk was ready to do twice the speed limit to get home. He forced himself to drive at a safe speed. His pride refused to allow him to expose his desperation. Judging by the way Rocky had made him shake and beg without penetration, Jakk needed to know what it would be like to have the man inside him.

A groan rose and caught in his throat as he pulled into his driveway. Eric sat on the porch, waiting. Jakk wondered how long he had been sitting there. There was no way he knew where Jakk had been or when he would be home.

"Fuck. This is about to get awkward."

Rocky flashed him a sympathetic smile. "I can call a cab and find a hotel. It's no big deal."

It was, and it pissed Jakk off that Rocky could say it wasn't. He wanted to be with Rocky. They only had tonight before Rocky had to go home. He would be goddamned if Eric stole another fucking thing from him. "You're the one I want here." Jakk couldn't hold back the passion.

Rocky nodded at his obvious seriousness. "Okay. Do you want me to wait in the car and let you two talk?"

Jakk felt the incredulous expression overtake his face. "No. I've said everything I need to say to him."

"Okay." Rocky sounded unsure.

That had his anger skyrocketing. How dare Eric endanger anything else in Jakk's life? Hadn't he destroyed enough?

Together, they climbed from the car. Jakk handed Rocky his keys. "Go ahead and get settled. This won't take long."

Eric's gaze moved from Jakk to Rocky as they approached. Hatred flashed in his dark blue eyes. Rocky nodded as he passed, as if he had no reason to worry. It was odd and uncomfortable. Rocky used Jakk's keys and headed inside.

"I guess I know the real reason you dumped me."

Jakk's brow furrowed. "What in the fuck are you talking about? First off, you know exactly why we're over. Secondly, that's my new agent. You know, one I needed since your bullshit got me dropped by my old one."

Guilt touched Eric's features. He shifted from foot to foot. Jakk's chest hurt. He still knew what he saw in Eric. Eric was big and cuddly. Jakk used to think he was the sweetest man alive. Once upon a time, Jakk would have done anything for him. Now he had stepped over that line between love and hate. There was no going back.

"I didn't mean for that to happen."

Jakk knew that, but it didn't matter now.

At his silence, Eric shoved his hands in his pockets. "I'd hoped I could take you to dinner and try to talk about things."

Jakk held his silence and simply stared at Eric. There was no way Eric didn't see his fury.

Eric ran his hand through his dark hair—like he thought to tear it out. "I uprooted my whole goddamn life for you. The least you can do is have one fucking dinner with me. What am I supposed to do now? I built my entire life around you."

For a second, Jakk fought the guilt, but he hadn't been the one to destroy them. "You should've thought about that before taking a sledgehammer to everything we had."

"Everything we had? It's everything you have. Always has been." He motioned toward the house. "None of this has ever been mine, and I knew it every day. I knew I had no hope of ever being anything but your secret shame if I didn't do something."

"You agreed to everything. I told you how it would be. You knew staying quiet was temporary. As soon as I retired and had us set for life—"

"Bullshit!" The yell cut through the air, startling Jakk into silence. Eric looked more enraged than Jakk had ever seen him, and that said a lot. "You never once thought about me. You weren't pining for the day you didn't have to hide me. I was nothing but a convenient fuck, keeping you safe while keeping you fed. Fuck you for that."

Jakk flinched with every word. He knew he wasn't faultless. They had equally destroyed each other. That was exactly why it was well past the time for them to move on. He tried tempering his voice. "You're better off without me. I told you I'll get you set up in a place to live back home. Start over. Find someone worthy of you and who treats you the way you deserve. To my soul, I know it would've been me one day. But I asked too much and we're too broken now. I'm sorry I wasted your time."

Tears welled in Eric's eyes. He paced away. His shoulders expanded on a deep breath. He didn't look at Jakk. "You can tell yourself whatever it takes to sleep at night, but you never loved me. Every time you said it, it was a lie. Love doesn't look like this." He headed toward the driveway where his car sat. "Keep your fucking money. That's the only thing you love."

The bitterness and coldness rolling off Eric in waves made Jakk's chest hurt. Every day, he swung wildly between who was most at fault. Eric was right on one thing, though. Jakk did tell himself a lot of lies and performed a ton of mental gymnastics to validate his decisions with Eric. No matter how they had ended up here, they were over and there was no going back. Jakk just wished he didn't feel like such a bastard.

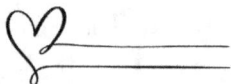

Rocky didn't move past the living room or take off his shoes. He shouldn't have gotten involved with someone this fresh out of a relationship. Love didn't die that fast. There was a real possibility he should just leave.

He should let Jakk's ex come inside and work things out. Rocky hated this feeling. He loathed knowing he made a stupid decision—again. Every time Rocky swore he would be smarter, he lied to himself.

Jakk came back inside, looking defeated. Despite all his alarm bells clanging, Rocky's heart squeezed. It was more than obvious Jakk blamed himself for this entire mess. Rocky understood. He, too, had lived with that guilty conscience before. Sometimes, there were no good choices. Jakk had killed himself to become the best, and it shouldn't matter he was gay, but it did. He had been put in an impossible position between the career he loved and the man he intended to spend his life with. What was he supposed to do?

It was on the tip of Rocky's tongue to suggest going to a hotel again. He couldn't leave Jakk like this.

Jakk looked his way. "I'm so sorry about all this."

"You have no reason to apologize."

Jakk's defeated expression somehow got worse. "I completely understand if you want to bail. I'm sure I look like a complete ass right now."

"What kind of friend would I be if I walked away on your bad days?"

A sweet smile touched Jakk's lips. "Probably a smart one."

The weight lifted from Rocky's chest. He was where he was supposed to be. Rocky patted the couch next to him. "Come, tell me how to make it better."

Rather than sitting where Rocky indicated, Jakk crossed the room and straddled Rocky. His mouth found Rocky's lips. Rocky's hands automatically slipped beneath the back of Jakk's shirt as he opened for Jakk. Every earlier doubt fled. Nothing mattered except the now. They were together.

"I need you inside me."

Rocky's stomach muscles clenched. His body responded like his dick was already in Jakk's hand. "Lead the way."

Jakk stood and pulled Rocky to his feet. Rocky held Jakk's hand on the way to his bedroom. The moment they crossed the threshold, Jakk whipped his shirt over his head and tossed it aside. Rocky followed his lead. He toed off his shoes and continued stripping while Jakk found condoms and lube. Rocky didn't even notice a single detail about the bedroom. All he saw was Jakk.

Once nude, Rocky crowded Jakk's space. He molded against Jakk's back and followed the waistband of his jeans with his hands until he reached the button. Rocky listened to Jakk's breathing turn ragged as he slid his zipper down. He swore he still felt Jakk's black mood lingering. That wasn't happening on his watch. Rocky shoved Jakk's pants down his hips, taking his underwear with them. With the slightest push, he had Jakk bent over the edge of the bed. Jakk completely surrendered. Rocky let his hunger grow as he lubed Jakk's hole and suited up. Jakk's body was so beautiful. Rocky never got tired of admiring it. But Rocky didn't think that was what caught him with Jakk. As angry as it made Rocky with himself, considering the bullshit from just five minutes ago, he wanted more with Jakk than sex. There was no chance this would end well.

Even the knowledge that this could only end in heartache didn't stop Rocky from lovingly stroking Jakk's back and ass as he led his cock to Jakk's hole. He took his time, teasing Jakk and stretching him.

"Please?"

The whispered plea nearly broke Rocky's brain. He thrust. His eyes fell closed as the heat engulfed him and Jakk's moan caressed his ears. He rocked inside him, savoring the sensations. It had been so long. Rocky had forgotten how good it felt to fuck. He couldn't lie to himself, though. Rocky had bent Jakk over this bed as punishment and to steal the intimacy from the moment. He wanted to remove his heart. Jakk intended to break it, and Rocky couldn't handle it.

Jakk pushed backward like he loved every second. "Yes. Fuck. Just like that."

A wave of sadness unexpectedly washed over Rocky. He wanted to be special. He was never special. Eric still owned Jakk's heart. He wasn't ready for Rocky. This was just...

nothing. Rocky didn't know if he spaced out or froze or both. He also didn't know how long he stood there—paralyzed with terror for his mental health. This would break him. He couldn't do this again. Rocky didn't know if he could survive this.

Rocky blinked, and he was on his back on the mattress with Jakk hovering over him.

"It's fine. Shhh. It's okay. We don't have to do this. I never meant to make you feel bad or used. I'm so fucking sorry."

Fuck. Rocky had checked out. He hadn't done that in ages. Then again, he hadn't had sex in ages either. He blinked. "I'm good."

Jakk looked defeated. He rolled onto his back and stared at the ceiling. "You're right to be upset. I don't deserve to have you here."

Goddamn it. Rocky was the one fucked in the head. Not Jakk. He didn't know how to say that, so an even worse confession escaped. "I like you way more than I should." Under any other circumstances, Rocky would have bitten off his tongue, but his mind was still hazy from the silent panic attack. "Nothing will come of this except me getting hurt." Fuck. Why couldn't he stop?

To his surprise, he found himself beneath a very pissed-off-looking Jakk. "What do you think is happening here? Do you think I'm the kind of guy who doesn't call the next day? Do you really believe I thought, 'I'll just fuck my new agent and we'll never speak on it again and everything will be good?' Is that really what you think?"

He couldn't believe they were having this argument nude, with Rocky still ready to go. Oddly, every angry word brought him back to life. "I think I'm a rebound and you'll realize it soon enough. When you do, the hurt will be my fault, because I knew I wasn't special, and I still couldn't wait to get hurt."

Jakk visibly deflated. "How can you think you're not special? Don't answer that. I know it's my fault." He kissed the corner of Rocky's mouth, lingering for a moment before pulling away again. "God, I don't want to have this discussion with you underneath me like this, but I can't let you leave this bed." He kissed the other corner of Rocky's mouth. "Eric started sleeping with someone else over a year ago. He said if I couldn't publicly claim him, then I shouldn't care if someone else did. I knew it was a way to try to force my hand, but it only made me realize I didn't love him anymore. We were still together, for my guilt's sake. Still, I didn't stray, and I didn't let him go. I don't know if that was pride or penitence. Either way, I'd watch him get ready to go out with someone else and I only felt relief."

Rocky's stomach was in knots. His gaze wouldn't waver from Jakk's expression. He told the truth. Whatever he had with Eric had died a long time ago. Still, Rocky didn't know how to feel. This wasn't how he pictured making love to Jakk would go.

"When sleeping with someone else didn't break me, you know what happened next. That's what I needed to finally let go of whatever kept me hanging on, but don't mistake that for love. He killed that a long time ago." His expression shifted. Light and life came back to his eyes. Rocky watched him transform from recalling a bleak existence to finding a spark. "Then you walked into my life." Rocky's breath caught. He was the reason Jakk looked happy again. "You can't know how much I want this. Not the sex, even though—goddamn." Yeah. Rocky got it. They were pretty fucking explosive together. Jakk smiled. It was so sweet and warmed Rocky's chest, carrying away the last of his doubts. "I want you. This isn't me looking for an escape or a healing balm to soothe my hurt and pride. I want you," he repeated with more intensity behind each word. "If I look angry at life or out of sorts, it's because I know this feels and looks like I can't possibly be serious. I'm enraged that I let Eric steal so much from me and now he gets to play the victim. It pisses me off that I met you right when everyone will think I'm hitting my whoring stage to deal with an ugly breakup. He left a long time ago. Since then, I've just been waiting for you."

Maybe it was bullshit. Rocky wasn't sure he cared. Every word Jakk spoke was what he needed to hear. He wasn't built to fuck and run. That was why he never bothered. He understood being with him was hard work, but he understood even more that no one wanted anything real any longer. Damned if Jakk didn't sound just like him—like anything less than real wasn't good enough.

Rocky rolled, pinning Jakk beneath him. He moved slowly, lowering his head. If Jakk wanted him to stop now, he would. Jakk lifted his head, meeting him halfway. Their tongues fought for control. It wasn't a sweet kiss. It was desperate. He scooped Jakk's leg from the bed, tucking his arm beneath it so he could control him. In an instant, he was back to root-deep in Jakk's ass. He kept Jakk held at the exact angle he wanted him and pumped inside him. Rocky knew what he was doing. Maybe it had been a long time, but he knew the exact angle to hit Jakk where it would drive him insane. The sounds vibrating around their entwined tongues proved his theory. Jakk swapped between scratching at the covers and tearing at Rocky's skin. Rocky didn't let up. He knew how to make Jakk fly, and he would. But Rocky hoped he got there quickly because Jakk's body felt too good. It had been too long. Rocky desperately wanted to pump cum into his ass, even if a condom would catch every drop. He needed to blow with his dick buried inside Jakk. It felt a lot like claiming him.

Jakk tore his mouth away and visibly fought for air. "Oh, God. I have to—" A loud cry tore from Jakk.

Rocky never looked away. He savored every second. Jakk's body convulsed, and Rocky lost his breath. He locked his back teeth and slammed himself inside Jakk over and over, driving himself to the edge. Then the world stopped as pleasure coursed through his veins. He was exactly where he should be.

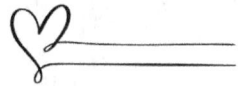

A smile kept pulling at Jakk's lips as he watched their fingers play. No one knew how fucking ecstatic he was. It was more than a post sex glow. They'd had a real adult conversation and there hadn't been anyone screaming. He had spoken his heart and Rocky had listened. They felt like they were headed somewhere. Even though Jakk hadn't seen this coming, he wanted them more than he dreamed possible. Rocky might have come from left field to sideswipe his life, but Jakk had never wanted anything more. He felt like he walked on clouds.

"I'll miss you when you leave tomorrow."

He felt Rocky smile against his temple. "I won't let that happen. Over the years,

I've gotten pretty fucking adept at being everywhere all at once. I'll figure things out."

Jakk couldn't stop grinning like an idiot. "You won't be the only one. I'm used to constant travel too. There's no way I'll let you sleep alone any longer than absolutely necessary."

For a moment, silence grew between them before Rocky finally broke it. "We're really doing this."

Jakk was every bit as shocked as Rocky sounded. He never expected to meet Rocky and get swept off his feet. Hell, he never expected to get swept off his feet, period. Yet here they were. He didn't regret a thing. "Damn right."

Rocky's arms tightened around him and—for once in a very long time—everything felt right. Tomorrow would bring a different set of problems.

He still had a team and the entire world set against him right now. Somehow, Rocky made all that feel manageable. Tomorrow would bring what it brought. Right now, he was exactly where he wanted to be.

Chapter Six

IT TOOK A FEW games and even more practices, but people started talking to him again. It started with one guy who had been his friend for years and then another. In the end, he learned Jayme was more pissed about feeling lied to than anything. Jakk didn't think he lied, exactly. He just hadn't been open. Jakk thought he was justified, considering how everyone reacted. It was a solid two months before everyone pretended nothing had happened. There was a small part of him that wanted to cling to his anger over their initial reaction, but that served no one. They were all in this game together. He just wanted to win.

Life with Rocky was another matter. It was easy. His entire life he had been told anything worth having was worth struggling for. Being with Rocky proved that wasn't the case. Everything was effortless. They somehow managed to spend at least every other night together. Splitting the traveling made things feel like nothing. He never expected things to feel so perfect.

Jakk tried to focus. He chewed on his mouth guard and paced the sideline. As soon as the whistle blew, he popped his mouth guard into place and threw on his helmet. On the twenty-yard line, he got into position. His gaze stayed locked on the man across from him. He barely heard the play being called. The moment the quarterback had the ball, Jakk shot through his opening. He didn't think. Jakk acted. He glanced over his shoulder just in time to see the ball sailing his way. His feet left the ground as he leapt upward. He tucked the ball against his body as a solid shoulder collided with his ribs. Despite getting taken down, he popped back up with a smile. He had picked up thirty yards. It had definitely been a good day for him. He hoped Rocky was somewhere watching. Jakk knew Rocky was in New York today, but that was all. A meeting had been pushed back from last night, stopping him from coming to see Jakk. Jakk missed him like crazy. He wanted to make Rocky proud.

They reset. Jakk found another opening. This time, he carried through, crossing that touchdown line. He tossed the ball into the stands before jumping up and chest-bumping Jayme. Everyone was all smiles as they jogged back to the sidelines. Fuck. It amazed him how doing everything for Rocky made him better. He wouldn't fail the man who showed up when everyone else turned their backs. This team was his co-workers. That was all. Nothing he did was for them. Everything was for the man he loved.

Jakk's thoughts screeched to a halt. Did he love Rocky? He had been with Eric for like eight months before realizing he loved the guy. Rocky and he had only been dating for two months. When had he fallen? Well, goddamn. He supposed he had better step up his game. One of these days, everyone would realize Rocky was more than his agent. When that day came, Jakk wanted Rocky to be proud as fuck to be with him. Nothing less would do.

"Everyone's partying at Emerson's nightclub tonight. You in?"

Jakk hesitated. Rocky wouldn't make it into town tonight either, and Jakk had a team meeting tomorrow, so he couldn't go to him. He needed to lean into the team's acceptance. "Sure. I'll be there."

The guy who asked smiled and jogged away.

Jakk bit back a sigh. The last thing he wanted to do was go to a nightclub, but what the hell? He had nothing better to do.

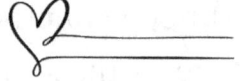

Countless screens played various games, catering to anyone there to see their team. Rocky leaned back in his chair, trying to get a good angle on Jakk's game. He felt itchy and impatient. Normally, it didn't bother him to meet with Oakley. Today, he just wanted to get back to Jakk.

"I hate to sound paranoid, but there's a dude who hasn't stopped staring at you since you sat down. Not in a good way."

Rocky focused on Oakley at the comment. His gaze was locked over Rocky's shoulder.

"I'll tell you when to look."

Rocky waited.

"Look now."

Rocky quickly checked over his shoulder. He couldn't hold back a groan. "For fuck's sake."

"I take it you know that guy?"

Rocky fought not to roll his eyes. "Honestly, I'm starting to think I need a restraining order. That's the guy I'm dating's ex. A few thousand miles from home," he tacked on, sounding bitter and explaining how wild this entire situation was.

Oakley's eyebrows rose. "You're dating someone? I hadn't heard."

Just the thought of Jakk had a smile snapping to Rocky's lips. "Yeah. Since I'm his agent—unethical, I know—I guess people haven't caught on."

"Who is this mystery man?"

"Jakk Johnson."

Oakley smiled. "Nice!"

Rocky snorted at his reaction. Oakley was one of those people who could be brooding one minute and a golden retriever the next. It was impossible not to like him.

"Why is his ex hardcore stalking you?"

Rocky made a helpless gesture. "Your guess is as good as mine. If no one else has figured out we're dating, I'm sure Eric has, or at least suspects." Rocky's gaze flickered toward the screen behind Oakley in time to see Jakk score. A shout escaped him before he could call it back. Luckily, it was a sports bar. His reaction wasn't uncommon.

Oakley glanced over his shoulder. "It looks like you signed a winner."

Rocky forced himself to focus on Oakley. He couldn't stop smiling. Jakk made him proud as hell. "Don't I always? I started with the best."

A wry smile touched Oakley's lips. "That was a long time ago. Now I'm old and slow. Not to mention in pain all the goddamn time."

Oakley wasn't old. Admittedly, he was past the prime for baseball, but age-wise, he wasn't old. "I can't imagine what you must think of me, then."

A bark of laughter burst from Oakley. He motioned for Rocky to get started. "Show me why we're meeting."

Rocky dug out his phone and leaned Oakley's way. He opened a PDF on the device and scrolled through the highlights of a contract for a sports convention appearance. It wasn't a ton of money, but he knew Oakley enjoyed the travel and the expenses were covered.

Oakley nodded along. His gaze slid over Rocky's shoulder again. "All that sounds good to me. Send it to me and I'll get it signed. Do you want me to take care of your little problem so you can get out of here without being followed?"

Rocky shoved his phone back in his pocket. "I won't pass on that deal. The quicker I get out of here, the faster I can get back to Jakk."

Oakley winked. "I've got you."

Rocky watched him stand and head Eric's way. On the sly, he looked on as Oakley accidentally on purpose bumped into Eric's table, tipping over a beer in his lap. The moment Eric was distracted by Oakley's profuse apologies and attempt to clean up his mess, Rocky made his break. He was out the door before Eric looked back up again. An evil smile pulled at his lips as he hailed a cab. It was time to get back to his man. He didn't want anything to slow him down. Fuck Eric. Jakk was his now. He wouldn't give him up.

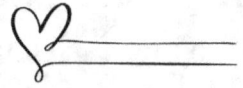

The nightclub was loud and the neon lights made Jakk's head hurt. He tried desperately to smile and enjoy himself. Instead, he couldn't stop thinking about how he hadn't heard from Rocky all day. Jakk didn't want to disturb him, in case he was still in meetings. The day had been a series of highs and lows. They had won. Everyone excitedly celebrated. Everywhere he looked, all Jakk saw were fake friends. Fake people. He didn't feel the same way about a lot of things any longer. There was no going back.

A beer appeared in front of his face. "I'm surprised you're not out there dancing with your team. Aren't you the reason they won?"

At the words spoken against his ear, Jakk spun. Rocky stood behind him. He was all smiles and travel mussed. He was fucking gorgeous. "You're here." His huge smile hurt his face. He was so fucking happy.

Rocky shook the beer at him. "You deserve this."

Jakk didn't give a fuck about the beer. He wanted to haul Rocky against him and take the kiss he craved. Instead, he caved to society and accepted the beer. "I thought you couldn't make it."

Rocky shrugged. He looked pleased with himself for getting the drop on Jakk. "Oakley can be an easy client when he's in the mood. He rushed so I could get back to you."

Something fluttered in Jakk's chest. "You told him about us?"

Rocky's expression changed. He looked uncomfortable. "Sorry. I didn't think to run that by you first. He won't say anything if you don't want anyone to know."

It hit Jakk. He didn't want to hide. Jakk was tired of fucking hiding. The worst had already happened. He wouldn't ruin this. "I'm fine with it if you are. It's not like we've hidden. It's not our fault people are blind."

Rocky snagged the collar of Jakk's shirt. "Maybe it's a little our fault." His mouth covered Jakk's.

Jakk immediately surrendered. He forgot where they were or that they could be seen. Nothing mattered except the tongue stroking his.

Rocky pulled away a hair. "Do you really want to be here?"

Jakk shook his head.

"I say we go home and celebrate properly."

Jakk nodded. There was nowhere he would rather be. He had found the one.

Chapter Seven

THEIR LEGS TANGLED BENEATH the covers. Jakk was the most comfortable he had ever been in his life. Rocky's nude body spooned his, keeping him warm and making it impossible for him to fully wake. Occasionally, his lips brushed Jakk's neck. A smile kept passing over Jakk's lips. He knew he should get up and face the day, but he wasn't ready. Jakk never wanted to leave Rocky's arms.

The alarm went off. A groan burst from Jakk. "No." He dragged the word out. "I don't want to go to work."

Rocky chuckled against his skin.

Jakk slapped the face of his phone to make it be quiet, but he didn't move. He was too content.

Rocky's hand slid across his hip. "How much time do you have?"

A hum vibrated in the back of his throat. Jakk could make time. "A couple of hours."

Rocky sucked his neck.

Jakk immediately went hard. That was his weakness. "Oh, God." He held Rocky's head lightly, silently begging for him not to stop.

Rocky didn't let him down. He stroked Jakk's erection. Even though Jakk felt how hard Rocky was for him, he made no move to do more than touch Jakk.

"Fuck. I've never seen anyone sexier when they're turned on. You could do porn."

A chuckle rose in Jakk's throat. He had never really thought about the way he looked. The laugh died when Rocky rolled, pinning Jakk beneath him. He disappeared just long enough to return with wet fingers. The cold lube swept down his crack and soaked his hole. Jakk held the sheet beneath him and buried his face in the mattress. He focused solely on feeling everything. That was the one thing Rocky did best: make him feel. Rocky bit his shoulder and licked his spine. When he drew Jakk's hips up and back, Jakk went willingly.

"So beautiful."

Unexpectedly, Jakk's throat swelled at the quietly spoken compliment. For a long fucking time, he had kept his heart on lockdown to keep from getting hurt while simultaneously feeling like nothing thanks to Eric and his bullshit. Life just felt so goddamn full of hope, and he felt desired again. Sometimes it was overwhelming. He was thankful he could hide his face. Jakk didn't want Rocky to stop. He likely would if he saw the way everything about him devastated Jakk—in the best of ways.

Rocky's cock stretched Jakk's asshole. "You make me feel like my whole life led to you."

Jakk couldn't breathe. His emotions were too high. Then Rocky thrust and Jakk forgot everything except the ecstasy. Moans vibrated from him. He was at complete peace with life as Rocky took him to the stars. When his orgasm hit, Jakk had to bite the sheet to stop himself from confessing his love. It was dumb. Realistically, they hadn't known each other that long. As Jakk listened to Rocky moan through his orgasm, they felt realer than anything he had ever experienced. He felt safe and alive. This was the real thing. Jakk never wanted this to end.

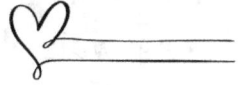

Jakk's team meeting was supposed to be a short one. Rocky didn't have much time. He wanted to do something special for Jakk. They had been together a couple of months and Rocky was happier than he had ever been. He was also exhausted. So fucking exhausted. He tried to hide how much the constant jump around the US and Canada affected him, but he was older than Jakk. This shit wore him down, forcing him to make a few decisions and adjustments. He had sat on the news until he had everything in order, but that day was today. Rocky wanted to set the mood.

He strolled through the store, going aisle by aisle. Despite being on a time crunch, he didn't want to miss anything. He had a list in his head. Rocky wanted the night to be perfect. His phone buzzed halfway through his shopping with Jakk, letting him know he was on his way home. With a silent curse, he picked up the pace. The last thing he wanted was for Jakk to beat him home. He grabbed the last of what he needed and rushed through the checkout. When he reached the car he borrowed from Jakk, his phone buzzed again.

Rocky jumped behind the wheel before checking his phone. His brain screeched to a halt. His lungs ceased to function. Rocky stared at the first of a stack of images.

Unknown number: *He gave up a good man for a whore.*

Image after image showed Rocky with someone else. Sometimes they were simply sitting too close. Other pictures were fake. Some were old and of things he was highly ashamed of doing. Strung together, they looked damning as hell.

Unknown number: *Yes, I sent these to him.*

Rocky blinked. His brain screeched back to life. He didn't bother responding or blocking the number. Nothing mattered more than getting to Jakk before he got it in his head Rocky would cheat. Fucking Eric. Rocky knew full well that was who sent those pictures. Eric was the one who had given Jakk a deep-seated fear of being with someone unfaithful. He had some fucking nerve. The images from the past and the ones of him getting close to go over contracts weren't the ones that scared him, even though those were horrible. He didn't know how to explain the fake pictures of him kissing other men. What the actual fuck? This was a nightmare. His worst fucking nightmare.

He one thousand percent believed he had met the man he was meant to spend the rest of his life with, and now this. Rocky thought he might hyperventilate. He didn't know what to do. There was a real possibility Jakk would toss him out before he even said a word. He couldn't survive the humiliation twice in one life. Rocky had spent years working his ass off to get out from underneath the stigma of people thinking a player could just fuck him to get a good contract. A free ride through life. Throw on a little charm and Rocky would do anything. Get what they want and then bounce. He was easy to manipulate like that. Goddamn it. Rocky slapped the steering wheel. For once, that wasn't the case, but it would fucking look that way when Jakk dumped him. He had kissed Jakk publicly last night. By now, everyone knew they were together. He couldn't do this again.

By the time he reached Jakk's place, he was in full-blown panic mode. Jakk's car already sat in the garage. Rocky parked Jakk's sports car in its usual place in the third bay. Even though he couldn't breathe, Rocky still grabbed the bags from the store. It was like he went through the motions without any help from his brain. Jakk was in the kitchen as Rocky came through the door. He turned as Rocky stepped into the room.

Rocky didn't give him a chance to toss him out. "I can explain." He dropped the bags.

Jakk looked down as they fell. "Okay."

Rocky pulled out his phone and opened the images as he closed the distance between them. He pointed toward the first one. "This is just me showing a client a contract on my phone. I didn't see any point in printing it since we met at a bar." He scrolled to the next one. "This is an old picture.

If you look, I'm still wearing my college championship ring." His breathing got more ragged-sounding as he went. It had been a long time since he had this big of an anxiety attack. "This one, I didn't think I'd be able to explain, but it's clearly us kissing, but someone has photoshopped a different face over yours. And this one—"

Jakk pushed the phone away and took Rocky's face between his hands. "Take a breath. Tell me what the fuck is going on."

Rocky numbly handed him the phone. He watched as Jakk flipped through every horrible image.

Finally, Jakk handed back the device. "Baby, I never got those. Even if I had, I'm not stupid. I know how manipulative Eric is, and I know you're not him."

Rocky's head swam. He felt unsteady on his feet. He wondered if he would drop. "You believe me?"

A sweet smile touched Jakk's lips. "I'm completely in love with you. It'll take a hell of a lot more than some badly photoshopped pictures to make me walk away."

The complete swerve from thinking he would lose Jakk to hearing Jakk say he loved him was his undoing. Thankfully, a stool at the island was close enough to catch him when his knees failed. He sat down hard. His gaze never wavered from Jakk. He had no idea how he looked, but Jakk shifted from foot to foot nervously.

"You're kind of making me feel like I should've kept that to myself."

That was enough to rally a few of Rocky's brain cells. "I hired someone to take over the travel part of my job."

Jakk blinked at the wild swing of subjects like he didn't realize they were talking about the same thing. "Okay." He blinked again, as if not fully recognizing the extent of what Rocky said. "You won't be traveling anymore?"

Rocky shrugged. "Well, I'll still have to travel occasionally, but nothing like I have been."

"We get to have more time together?"

"If you'd like." He didn't want to assume anything.

Jakk shuffled closer. "You did that for me?"

Fuck. He felt so goddamn vulnerable. Jakk could crush him now. "Yeah. I also did it for me. I hate being away from you. You make me feel something I never thought I would again, but I'm equally sure I've never felt this much. I love you."

Jakk looked like he might cry as his hands landed on Rocky's shoulders. His gaze never wavered from holding Rocky's stare. "Stay here with me."

Rocky's brow furrowed. "I am."

Jakk licked his lips, looking nervous. "I mean permanently."

The request was a big one. They had just exchanged I love yous. It was a big jump from that to living together. Rocky couldn't imagine ever sleeping apart.

"You don't have to answer right now." He took a step back. His gaze slid away. "What all did you get at the store?" Jakk's voice was a bit too cheery.

Rocky realized his slow responses hurt Jakk. He never wanted that. "I grabbed what I need to make you a romantic dinner. Things took a turn when I got that text, but I wanted everything to be perfect for when I told you about my plans for work. Now it can just be a celebration of us moving in together."

Jakk's gaze snapped to his. "Are you sure? I never want to pressure you. Knowing you love me is enough. We're too important to me to do anything to—"

Rocky stood and kissed Jakk, cutting off his nervous chatter. He knew all that and more. Rocky was well aware he could say no and Jakk wouldn't pressure him. He knew they would be okay, no matter what. It had just taken Rocky a moment to process, but he wanted this and more. He craved experiencing everything with Jakk. They were perfect together. There was no such thing as too much or too soon. They were a set.

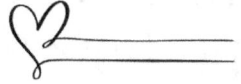

Jakk watched Rocky cook with a mixture of elation, wonder, and rage. He was so in love. How dare Eric try to ruin anything else for Jakk? The fucking nerve. It wasn't even good Photoshop and Eric had been taking digital art classes, for fuck's sake. If he wanted, he could have made those images impossible to differentiate from reality. He hadn't even bothered. It was obvious he thought Jakk was dumb and easily manipulated. Maybe he had been when they were together. Those days were gone. Rocky was his. Jakk wouldn't lose him.

He still couldn't believe Rocky had hired someone so they could spend more time together. Jakk was even more shocked Rocky had agreed to move in. Rocky had said he loved Jakk. He was over the moon. Jakk couldn't handle not touching him for another second. He stood and crowded Rocky's space. Jakk pressed his lips against Rocky's shoulder blade and held on while Rocky continued cooking, like he hadn't acquired a leech on his back.

Rocky chuckled when Jakk kept step with his every move without letting go. He bit back a sigh when his phone buzzed in his pocket. Jakk regretfully let go and dug out the device.

Private Number: *Good strategy, fucking Rocky to land the best contracts.*

Jakk's eyebrows shot up at the text. He had no clue who sent it or why they would say such a thing.

Jakk: *Who is this?*

Private Number: *Just a colleague wanting to send my congrats. Sometimes you have to take a dick up the ass to get ahead. Everyone knows Rocky will do anything for a blow job. We've all been there.*

"What the fuck?"

Rocky turned. His gaze dropped to Jakk's phone before moving to hold his stare. "What's up?"

With no clue where to start, Jakk handed Rocky the phone. He studied Rocky's expression as he read the exchange. Rocky just looked sad as he passed the device back to Jakk. Rocky went back to cooking, confusing Jakk.

"How do I respond to that?"

"I can't decide that for you." Rocky's voice sounded dead.

Jakk quickly blocked the mystery messenger before setting the phone aside. He crowded

Rocky's space again, clinging to him as he had earlier. "Talk to me. What's going on?"

He felt Rocky shrug. "It seems someone is trying to break us up, and it's looking more and more every second like it's working."

That remark doubled Jakk's confusion. "Please, just leave that for a second and look at me."

At his demand, Rocky set his spatula aside and turned. Jakk sucked in a breath. He looked wrecked. Jakk turned off the stove and took Rocky's hand. He led him to the living room and urged him to sit before straddling him so he couldn't get away.

With his arms wrapped around Rocky's neck, Jakk toyed with the ends of his hair while holding his stare. "I can't help if you won't tell me what's going through your mind."

"They weren't lying."

Jakk's stomach dropped. "What do you mean?"

Rocky swallowed so hard, it looked like it hurt. "When I first started out as an agent, I was determined to succeed, but I was also kind of a mess."

Having experienced the same rejection as Rocky, Jakk understood that. "That's fair."

"It sort of made me an easy target, I guess, but I also let it happen."

An ugly picture unfolded in Jakk's mind. Rocky had lost his dream and was vulnerable. He represented men who would do literally anything for their big break. Jakk wondered how many men had used and humiliated him before Rocky shut down and stopped trusting everyone. He wondered if Rocky thought Jakk was one of them. Obviously, other people thought exactly that. At least one person out there did, anyhow.

"You know I'm not one of those guys, right? You know this is real, don't you?"

Rocky never wavered from holding his stare. "The intelligent side of me knows the truth. I guess there's still just a small piece of me that's scared shitless." He swallowed again. "I can't go through all that again."

Damn. Jakk had leaned so hard on Rocky from day one. He hadn't realized he wasn't the only one drowning. "How crazy do you want me to get to prove myself? I can get pretty fucking insane."

One corner of Rocky's mouth lifted. It was obvious he didn't want to doubt them. "Every day I wake up and you're still around, you've proven yourself. This isn't your issue. It's mine. I never wanted you to feel like I doubt you." His expression turned defeated.

"I also don't want you to think I'd use my position as your agent to get you in bed or keep you in check."

"Okay. You're fired."

Rocky looked as if Jakk slapped him.

He realized immediately that was the wrong strategy. "You're rehired. Let's get married." Yeah, even Jakk couldn't believe what he said. He heard himself. The words had simply popped out. But then, he didn't stop. "I won't have anyone questioning my love for you, especially you. You're mine. More than that, you're the best thing that's ever happened to me. That has nothing to do with your fucking job, or mine, for that matter. Yeah, you showed up and rescued me when everyone else turned their backs, but my career isn't what you saved that night. It was me. My sanity and my heart. I was silently falling apart before you. There's nothing I won't do to prove I just want you."

The way Rocky stared at him with hope bleeding from his eyes swelled Jakk's chest. This was love. If anyone thought otherwise, they were dumb and blind.

"I don't doubt you."

Jakk gave him a sharp nod. "I don't doubt you either. The moment you want to say yes, just tell me. I'm completely set to spend the rest of my life with you."

A sweet smile touched Rocky's lips. "I love you."

"I love you too." Jakk kept the words matter of fact. He needed Rocky to take this seriously.

"I should finish dinner before it's ruined."

"In a second." Jakk pressed a sweet kiss to Rocky's lips. "Now you can go."

The smile that lit Rocky's face made every second of his life worthwhile. They both had a past, and it was obvious everything they had left behind wanted its pound of flesh. It wouldn't be happening. This was real. They were solid. Jakk would be damned if anyone broke them.

Chapter Eight

ROCKY: *THE MOVERS JUST pulled away and I'm doing a final walkthrough with the cleaning crew. Then I'll be on my way.*

Jakk: *I just left practice and am headed home now. So I'll definitely have no trouble getting to the airport in time to pick you up. Were they able to get your car and everything? Do we need to make any trips back?*

Rocky: *They're towing the car behind the truck. I'll need to come back again to finalize the sale and all that, but otherwise that's it and you know—even when I have to be here—I always come running back to you. You're my new home now.*

Jakk*: Mmm. I love the sound of that.*

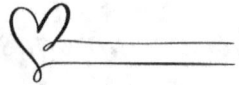

Jakk*: Practice ran late and I'm running behind. Remind me what you needed from the store.*

Rocky: *I was just about to text you. I ended up getting a delivery so you wouldn't have to make an extra stop. All I need is you.*

Jakk: *You always have that.*

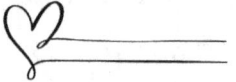

Rocky: *I can't believe it's already the final game of the playoffs. Good luck. You know I'm always rooting for you.*

Jakk: *I can't believe how fast the last five months have gone with you. It feels like just yesterday when you rushed to the rescue after that first game of the season. No matter what happens tonight, these have been the best months of my life.*

Rocky: *Same.*

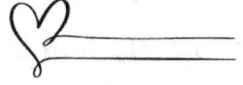

Eric stared at the enormous screen, taking up most of the wall across the bar. It was fitting to see Jakk this way—larger than life. That was how Eric had always seen him. From day one, Jakk had been nothing more than a dream—one Eric had always been destined to wake from. He could still recall the exact moment he had realized the spark in Jakk's eyes had been desire, and it was directed at him. His stomach had dropped to his feet. He had been completely terrified of taking a chance on that guy—the popular one. The closeted one. Then Jakk had kissed him and Eric had been completely lost. His heart hadn't stood a chance. Then Jakk had entered the draft and landed a multi-million-dollar contract along with several sponsorships. At first, when Jakk had said Eric would be coming with him, Eric had been filled with so much hope. He had honestly believed that was it. Jakk had made it big, and the moment had come he would no longer be the secret. Eric had been so wrong—so painfully mistaken. Now, he was the villain. It was almost laughable. He was the one who lost everything, yet he was at fault. All the years of silent suffering meant nothing. Everything about the situation was a tough pill to swallow. But the worst part was this: the goddamn longing. For the rest of his life, he would get to watch Jakk conquer the world while he still ached alone. He couldn't lie and say desperation hadn't driven him down some dark paths. Eric had lied and manipulated, praying Jakk would finally just be his, but not for one second did he deserve this. Still, he couldn't tear his gaze from Jakk on the screen, snow falling in steady fluffy flakes while Jakk looked completely unbothered by the cold. Strong. Sexy. Forever lost to Eric.

"My friend isn't coming, so you're wasting your time."

The claim pulled Eric from his spiraling thoughts. A guy who looked vaguely familiar hovered over his table, but no matter how he searched his mind, the guy's words didn't make sense.

"Cool, I guess."

He pulled out a chair and sat. His ridiculously light eyes stayed locked on Eric in a very uncomfortable way—almost as if he tried to intimidate him. "What's the point in stalking him, anyhow?"

Eric had never been more confused, and that was saying a lot. "What in the fuck are you talking about?"

"This is the second time you've been here."

Eric's confusion grew. "Okay." That was an odd thing to say because Eric came here all the time. A memory suddenly washed over him. "You're the guy who spilled a beer on me."

His mouth lifted in one corner, making him look wicked as hell and letting Eric know that drink had been purposeful. "Like I said, you're stalking my friend."

Now that Eric recognized him, Eric knew exactly who he meant. "Rocky Zeal? The agent? Why would I bother stalking him?"

The first hint of discomfort lit the man's features. "Well, I mean, you don't live here in New York and he's dating your ex. You don't think it's a little strange for you to turn up where he does?"

"He's dating Jakk?"

The guy's gaze slid away. There was no missing the pain in Eric's question.

Eric fucking hated this continuous looking like a needy fool. He took a breath and squared his shoulders. "As it happens, I do live here. I'm sure most people don't realize that—since I gave up every goddamn thing to be with Jakk—I lost everything when he kicked me to the curb. Since I have absolutely nothing now, I had to come here to live with my aunt. She's the only family I have left with room for me. This place is the closest sports bar where I can watch Jakk's games without being pitied or judged. Well, it was before today, anyhow."

The more Eric spoke, the more the man across from him softened. That was good. Eric was so fucking exhausted by everyone's anger and hatred. He was just tired, period. To his surprise, the guy held out his hand. "I'm Oakley."

Despite his desire to be alone, Eric shook. "Eric."

Oakley nodded and then motioned toward a nearby server, asking for two more drinks. Eric bit back an inner sigh. It seemed he wouldn't get to peacefully wallow today. That was a fucking shame.

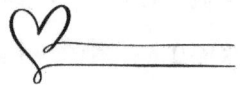

The excitement was high and the chatter nonstop as everyone showered. They had won the division. Rocky was too impatient to see Jakk. He was thrilled and proud as hell. No one could say Rocky had been thinking with his dick when he signed Jakk. Jakk was fucking amazing on the field. He was just as fantastic off the field too, but that was another story. Today had completely been Jakk's day. He had won this game. Everyone knew it, especially Rocky. He couldn't get to his man quickly enough.

Rocky saw Jakk near his locker. He didn't make it two steps in his direction before someone stepped in his path.

"Hey, Rock. How have you been?"

His face greeted Jayme before his mouth. It was too late, but Rocky still tried to call his hate-filled expression under control. "I'm great. Excuse me." He tried to keep moving. Rocky didn't want to chat. He didn't want to know how Jayme's life was going.

Jayme didn't let him pass. "I was hoping we could talk sometime."

As Jayme made the claim, Rocky locked eyes with Jakk. The words sank in, and Rocky's gaze snapped back to Jayme. He couldn't stop the disgust from pulling at his features. "No." He stepped around Jayme and headed for Rocky. The way Jakk's eyebrows rose made Rocky realize how enraged he must look. He tried rearranging his features. When he reached Jakk's side, he didn't have to fake it. He was happy as hell.

"Hey, baby. You did it!"

Jakk smiled. He stole a quick kiss. "What was all that with Jayme?"

Rocky shrugged it off. "He wanted to talk shop, and all I wanted was to get to you. I honestly didn't mean to look so irritated."

For a moment, Jakk simply stared at him without responding. In the silence, Rocky knew Jakk saw everything. Jayme had been one of the clients to use him. Rocky had dropped him once he had realized.

A sad smile tugged at Rocky's lips. "Please let it go."

Jakk's hardened features softened. His gaze moved over Rocky's face. "If that's what you want. Everyone is headed to Emerson's nightclub again to celebrate. Are you game, or would you rather go home?"

He would rather go home. Rocky couldn't say that. This was Jakk's moment. "This is your night. Your team probably wants to make sure you know they're not oblivious. This game was all you."

Jakk shrugged and pulled on a shirt. "Not really. I can't do shit without a good quarterback and protection. Nothing is ever just one person in sports."

He was so humble. Rocky was so in love. There would never be anyone more perfect for him. No one could make him happier. "I'd like to accept your offer."

Jakk froze in the middle of grabbing his bag. His gaze moved to hold Rocky's stare. He didn't play dumb, but he also didn't assume anything. "Is that a yes to my marriage proposal?"

Rocky slowly nodded. "That's a yes."

"Woot!"

Rocky startled at the sudden shout.

Heads turned their way as Jakk grabbed Rocky and hauled him in for another kiss. He wore a huge grin as he pulled away and pointed at Rocky. "He's marrying me!"

To his shock, Rocky's face heated. People congratulated them. He had no idea why he blushed. It was a bit like getting the birthday song sung to him in the middle of a crowded restaurant. He didn't know where to look or what to say. Thankfully, Jakk had his hand and led him out before he melted to the floor.

Jakk had driven to the stadium. Rocky had come later in an Uber. Now, all Rocky had to do was sit in the passenger seat and disappear inside his thoughts. He had really just done that. Rocky had agreed to marry Jakk. Jakk hadn't even considered keeping it a secret. Wow. Jakk genuinely loved him. It felt fucking amazing.

Rocky swore he only blinked and Jakk pulled into their garage. "What happened to going to Emerson's?"

Jakk flashed him a smile. "Truthfully, I didn't really want to go. Then you gave me something even better to celebrate."

Rocky leaned his head back against the headrest and stared at Jakk. He was beautiful. "You should probably forgive your teammates one of these days. It's obvious they're trying."

Jakk killed the engine before meeting his stare. "No. They're not. Not really. I'm unabashedly living my life whether they accept it or not. What you see is them having no choice if they want me to help them win. That's not real acceptance. Not that it matters." He opened the door and climbed from the car, leaving Rocky to follow suit. "I no longer care what they think. They're my coworkers. That's it. You're the love of my life. You're the only opinion that matters."

"Well, aren't we a pair of bitter bitches?"

Jakk chuckled as he unlocked the door. "Nah. We're just living for each other. There's nothing wrong with that." Jakk turned as they entered the house. He walked backward and held Rocky's hips. "And I fully intend to live for you."

He already did. Rocky saw it every day. He closed the gap between them and stole this kiss he wanted. "Thank you for loving me."

The words came out in a whisper. Rocky couldn't help it. Jakk kept him moved. No one else could love him better.

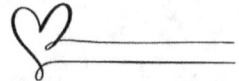

Jakk rode a high he couldn't even put into words. Everything he had worked toward slowly became a reality and then there was Rocky. When Jakk had popped the question, it had been a heat of the moment kind of thing. Now that some time had passed, and Jakk had time to think, he wanted to spend the rest of his life with Rocky with the power of seven suns. Rocky agreeing to marry him was everything.

Jakk held up one finger. "Just wait right here for a second."

Rocky looked confused, but he didn't budge as Jakk rushed down the hall. He dug through his dresser until he found the box he had stashed. Jakk skipped down the hall like a kid, making his way back to Rocky. Rocky's bright smile made his antics worthwhile.

"Are you completely sure you want to marry me?"

Rocky's expression softened. "Of course."

Jakk gave him a sharp nod. "Good." Jakk popped open the box and pulled the ring from inside. "Then I'd love it if you wore this." Rocky's shock had Jakk ready to pat himself on the back. Two days after proposing, Jakk had bought Rocky a ring. He wanted to be prepared if Rocky actually said yes. Now he was grateful as hell for his forethought. Rocky looked moved beyond words.

Jakk slipped the ring onto Rocky's hand. Something moved inside his chest as he did. The moment was more powerful than even he expected. His throat swelled. This was really happening. When his chin lifted and their eyes met, Jakk's breath caught. Rocky felt as much as Jakk. It was in his eyes. This was real love. They equally wanted to spend the rest of their lives together.

His phone rang. Jakk's shoulders fell. There was always a distraction around every corner. He checked his phone. "It's Mom."

"I'll grab us drinks."

They shared a quick kiss and headed in opposite directions. While Rocky went to the kitchen, Jakk moved to the couch. He answered as he sat.

"Hello?"

"Hey, baby. I saw your game. Congratulations! You did amazing."

"Thank you."

"I tried to wait as long as possible to call so I wouldn't catch you at the stadium, but you know me. It's almost my bedtime."

"I'm home. So it's fine."

"Good. That gives us time to talk." A smile snapped to Jakk's lips. She would have talked no matter what, and they both knew it. His mom kept going, proving his thoughts. "I ran into Eric last week at the store. He was in town visiting his mom in memory care. It's so sad. He's been through so much."

Jakk swallowed his annoyance. "You know we broke up a while back, Mom."

She sighed. "I know, but you two were together for so long, and you were so cute together. A part of me keeps hoping you'll work things out. You were all he had."

Fuck. He wished everyone would stop making him feel guilty for doing what was best for himself for once. "Actually, I've been dating someone else for a while now, and I've asked him to marry me. He said yes."

Silence met his confession. It dragged on before his mom finally broke it. "Were you cheating on Eric?"

Jakk rolled his eyes. "No, Mom. I wasn't cheating on Eric. You know things weren't good for a long time. I had time to grieve us before we even ended. If anyone should understand that, it's you." It was a bit of a crappy thing to say. His parents' marriage had been ugly for years before his mom finally filed for divorce. Then his dad had died of a widow maker before anyone even learned they had split. Mom had gotten his life insurance, and everything had worked in her favor. She shouldn't fault him for wanting to be happy again.

"What's his name?"

Jakk released the breath he had been holding. "Rocky. He's a sports agent."

"Oh. Is this the same guy who rushed to your rescue?"

He automatically smiled. "It is. You'll love him."

"You're my son. I'm always on your side, so I'm sure I will. We need to talk about Christmas. If he's coming, I need to get him a gift. I don't want him sitting around watching everyone else open presents."

His mom always came through. "He'll be there." Rocky appeared in the doorway. Jakk's eyes immediately followed his every move as he crossed the room to sit with Jakk. "When are we doing it this year?" They always waited and celebrated Christmas in January, since Jakk's game schedule always made it nearly impossible for him to go home for any length of time that mattered. They liked to spend time together. That didn't happen if Jakk had to rush right back to Minnesota.

His mom started talking about dates and explaining her reasoning when comparing it with his schedule, since they had made it past the playoffs. This year, it looked like things would be pushed all the way to the end of February or March. He listened as Rocky played with his fingers. It hit him exactly how perfect life felt. Quiet. Peaceful. It was nice. They were everything he hadn't known he had been searching for. Jakk brought Rocky's hand to his mouth and kissed it. For the first time, life felt completely flawless.

Chapter Nine

İT WAS HARD TO believe it had been a year since Jakk first touched him and put Rocky out of his misery. They were back to where it all started in Pickering. The same party went on around them. Just as much alcohol flowed. Rocky still couldn't take his eyes off Jakk. That was also the safest way to avoid Storm's constant I-told-you-so looks. That was fine. Storm had obviously seen something between them the first time he met Jakk. Rocky was so fucking grateful he hadn't been wrong.

Jakk slowly moved with him on the dance floor, keeping time with the music. Their wedding was right around the corner, and they needed this break. Despite having hired someone to handle everything, there was still a lot of stress that went into a big wedding. Rocky would have been happy with something small or even just them with a justice of the peace. Jakk was the one who insisted the world see their love. Sometimes Rocky wondered if Jakk even realized how much he changed from the man who hadn't wanted anyone to know about his sexuality. More than that, Rocky wondered if Jakk understood how every decision he made proved how right Rocky had been to give him a chance. No one could possibly understand how terrified he had been of Jakk. He was so fucking grateful he hadn't missed out on this life.

Rocky automatically tightened his hold on Jakk at just the thought of not having this.

Jakk's lips brushed his collarbone. "You good?"

Rocky smiled at the question. Jakk always worried about him. "Perfect, actually."

He felt Jakk smile against his skin. "Could I make you more perfect?"

"I mean, you could try."

Jakk's body shook with laughter, making Rocky's smile grow. "Okay. I have an idea." He took Rocky's hand and led him off the dance floor. Rocky was onboard as soon as Jakk headed upstairs to their bedroom. He never got enough of Jakk.

Jakk led him to the bed. "Sit."

Rocky did as told. His smile never wavered. He hoped Jakk was getting ready to do a strip show or something. There was nothing sexier than Jakk's nude body.

Jakk moved to his overnight bag and came out with a magazine. A hint of confusion creeped in, but Rocky stayed put. Jakk sat cross-legged on the bed and flipped through the magazine before passing it Rocky's way opened to a specific page. "This is an early edition."

Rocky checked the front. It was a big name sports magazine. He returned to the article. There was a page-sized image of Jakk in uniform on one page. On the other, there was an interview. Rocky read. There were the usual stats and praise of Jakk's performance last season. From there, things got personal.

Interviewer: Talk to us about your fiancé.

Jakk: Sure. What would you like to know?

Interviewer: I think a lot of people were surprised for you to move so quickly from the controversy of your outing to announcing your engagement. What happened?

A look of wonder passes over Jakk's features. He shrugs. Jakk: I guess when you've met the one, you know it. Rocky and I started out with everything in common and a fast friendship. From day one, it was like we had known each other forever. I was under a lot of stress and dealing with a huge sense of betrayal. Rocky got that. He was there. Honestly, he's my best friend and I can't marry him fast enough.

Rocky's throat swelled. Tears swam in his eyes, but he kept reading.

Interviewer: For those who don't know, Jakk is set to marry Rocky Zeal this October. Rocky is a highly sought after sports agent and retired professional basketball player. The only question I have left is, are we invited to the wedding, and will there be an open bar?

Jakk: {laughing} You're welcome to come, Chuck, but it'll be a closed event otherwise, and yes. There'll be an open bar.

Interviewer: You might just see me there. Let Rocky know I said congratulations on your upcoming nuptials.

There was more, but Rocky only skimmed the rest. He was moved beyond words. He met Jakk's stare. His throat didn't want to work. His voice came out sounding scratchy. "Thank you for this."

Jakk looked confused. "Why are you thanking me?"

It hit Rocky. Everything Jakk did was purely out of love. He didn't realize how he saved Rocky every day. His genuine love wiped away every terrible memory from his past.

"For loving me," Rocky said, for lack of a better explanation.

Jakk took the magazine and set it aside before crawling Rocky's way and tumbling him onto his back. He straddled Rocky's body. "You never have to thank me for loving you. That's literally the easiest thing I've ever done. Now, give me my kisses."

A laugh burst from Rocky at Jakk's growly-sounding demand. "Come get them."

"Challenge accepted." Jakk shifted positions, molding against Rocky. His arousal couldn't be missed as their bodies met. The heated expression Jakk wore as he lowered his head had Rocky ready to beg for more than sex. He wanted their forever to look just like this. Rocky needed every one of Jakk's kisses. Most of all, Rocky wanted Jakk for the rest of their lives. There was no greater blessing.

Keep an eye out for the next Sporting Pride, *Catching Him*.

Please consider leaving a review at the retailer where you purchased this book. Reviews really help with a book's visibility, which allows me to continue writing more stories. Thank you, Charity.

About the Author

CHARITY PARKERSON IS AN award-winning and multi-published author with several companies. Born with no filter from her brain to her mouth, she decided to take this odd quirk and insert it in her characters. One of her greatest loves is writing morally gray characters. You'll find them scattered throughout her hundreds of titles.

*Nine-time Readers' Favorite Award Winner

*2015 Passionate Plume Award Finalist

*2013 Reviewers' Choice Award Winner

*2012 ARRA Finalist for Favorite Paranormal Romance

*Five-time winner of The Mistress of the Darkpath

Connect with her online:

*Sign up for her newsletter: https://bit.ly/charityparkersonnewsletter

*Join her readers' group on Facebook: http://bit.ly/CharitysTribe

* W e b s i t e : https://www.charityparkerson.com

*A list of her social media accounts and giveaways all in one place: http://hy.page/charityparkerson

www.ingramcontent.com/pod-product-compliance
Lightning Source LLC
Chambersburg PA
CBHW070936250626
47159CB00009B/3276